SHATTER

A Collection of Poetry

Taylor Juarez

ISBN (e-book): 979-8-9876890-0-4
ISBN (paperback): 979-8-9876890-1-1

Cover design by: Taylor Juarez

Printed in the United States of America

To the one who sets my soul on fire.

Introduction

Ten years ago, I created an anonymous Tumblr blog and began writing poetry. At the time, my anonymity allowed me to be uninhibited with my writing. I could pour out my thoughts and feelings without worrying what people thought of me. Writing became necessary to my survival. It was the way I made sense of my life and the world around me. Over the years, I gained many followers and enjoyed being part of the online writing community. As I grew older, it became clear that writing was a huge part of who I was - and I was keeping it hidden. I realized that it was time to put my name on my work and reveal my identity. I'll admit, it was very daunting to reveal my most vulnerable thoughts to those who knew me. But the more I wrote, the braver I became. I have learned that suffering and feeling in silence doesn't make me stronger. It only makes me more afraid of being who I am. There has been so much freedom in the sharing of my work. In the acceptance of my true self. I am so excited to finally be putting all the pieces together and publishing my very first book of poems. The last decade of my life has been a shattering, an awakening. This book explores my journey through darkness and light, through joy and pain, and embraces the mess and the chaos that will always be part of me. This book is my becoming. Read me. Understand me. This is who I am.

From this pedestal
I look down
at all those I am
afraid to disappoint.
What will they think
if they see
all the broken pieces
hidden underneath?
From up here
I maintain the image
of a life well-kept
an image I dare not shatter.
But what if this perfect image
is not what they
care to see?
What if the real obstacle
has always been me?
What I'm learning of suffering
is there is healing in the telling
and the people who love me
will accept me with open arms
the moment I let go
and let my feet touch the ground.

I may appear quiet
but pay attention
and you'll hear me
screaming onto the page.
Look closely
and you'll see
all that I reveal
because I am not
afraid of the truth.
I write better than I speak
so if you want to know me
find me in the ink.

Silence and solitude
when given a chance
speak the loudest truths.
Slow down and surrender
sink into the stillness
open yourself to the answers
you desperately seek.
Let the dust settle
look to the sky
and you will begin to understand
all the reasons why.

We have always been
friendship on fire
love built upon
endless conversations
and everyday experiences.
There's always been
a deep understanding
of who the other one is
how our similarities align
and our differences complement.
Through the best and the worst
we've cultivated our strength.
We've formed a bond
through a collection of comforts
vulnerability shared effortlessly
desire steadfast like the moon.
Though it may wax and wane
even when we can't see it
it's always there.

There's something about
the stillness
the calming silence
that settles our minds.
There's magic in the unspoken
the language that
only we know.
One glance
and our eyes understand.
A gentle touch
and we know home.
This serenity is timeless
the bridge that will
always exist between us.
No matter where we go
we will always meet here.

Everywhere we turn
we burn and burn
as our rights get overturned.
Fear, hatred, propaganda
corruption running so deep
it is destroying everything
we've worked for.
A country built on dreams
of freedom for all…
what a vicious lie.
Freedom for the rich.
Freedom for the powerful.
Freedom for a cruel minority
while the majority of us
remain imprisoned.
But our voices will not
be silenced.
The fight of our lives
has only just begun.
Let them burn it down
for we will rise
from the ashes.

Freckles scattered across the sky
a collection of tiny specks
some intense in their glow
some soft and subtle.
A sea of sparkles
in a deep black abyss
surrounding you
and pulling you into infinity.
A million little wonders
reminding you that beauty
can be found in darkness.

With the invention of clocks
we were put in a box
confined by the hands
that determined our fate.
We hear the sound
of time passing us by
a persistent reminder
of the minutes we are losing.
And yet there is comfort
in the repetition
of the cycle that holds us steady.
Relief in the fading of pain
hope embedded in the anticipation
of moments to come.

Your soft brown curls
slipping through my fingers
your fiery eyes longing
but filled with calm.
I feel it radiating
this energy we have.
The spark that's always
been there.
A whole world exists
between us
a whole life
that we've created.
I close my eyes
feel you move in closer
and I become infinite.

An ambassador of love
guiding me through this
never-ending maze of life
filled with wisdom
and a kindness that
warms me to my core.
She crafted so much
of my story
filled it with joy
created a space for
passion and wonder.
Always there to nurture
with an ear to listen
or a shoulder to cry on.
The older I get
the deeper my gratitude grows
for a mother that gave me
the ability to see
the magic in the mundane
and the drive to never
stop chasing it.

A trail of evidence
treasures packed away
in boxes on shelves
filled to the brim
with past versions of myself.
What a joy to sift through
photographs, letters, drawings,
so many tokens of the
life I have lived.
It's good to be reminded
of all the moments
worth living for,
all the stepping stones
along the way
that have given me
something to believe in.
We survive in
small, infinite moments
and that is how
we make a life.

Even as I sleep
you enter me
shaking the walls
of my restless mind
your love seeping in
taking over my psyche.
You take hold of me
and I feel your skin
warm and inviting
as you overwhelm
all my senses.
It feels so real
I gasp in my dreams
begging for more
until you start to slip away
and I awake breathless
the feeling of you
lingering on my skin.

A house of cards
a funhouse of mirrors
a carousel that never
stops turning.
I am surrounded by illusions
I marvel at the very things
that confound me.
I'm lured in by the wonder
but left wanting more.
Everywhere I turn
I see it.
I feel it.
I can't escape.
I hear the sounds faintly
the ghosts of childhood past
the innocent days
I can never get back.

Here it comes
crashing down again
as though we've been
playing a game of Jenga
on repeat.
Over and over
we stack up
and pull
and balance
trying to grow tall.
But the more we grow
the more fragile we become
as we see the foundation
disappearing before our eyes.
These pieces of our lives
always shifting,
so where do we
find our strength?

Always running
always chasing
always grasping
but the life I long for
is out of reach.
The memory of
the aliveness
haunting the shadows
of daily life.
So far gone
are the carefree days
the days when
everything seemed possible.
Reality is stifling
and although there
is still joy to be found,
it doesn't feel the same.
Life is a shell
of what it used to be.

We are all children
searching for joy
longing to fulfill
our most basic desires.
We are all children
wandering
wondering
wishing.
We grow up
we lose touch,
but underneath the
personas we've become,
we are still wanting.
We are all children
driven by the yearning for joy.

I always give the impression
that I have it all together.
People look at me
as though they are
looking into a still
body of water.
Everything seems
calm and controlled.
If only they knew
how I drown in my
own murky waters.
Calm is the illusion
I keep, when really
there is chaos hidden beneath.

It burns in me
this desire to be free
to reach the mountaintop
and shout to the skies
so the world can see
this is me.
I want to give all I have
to this life, to leave behind
a trail of words and films
and stories everywhere I go.
I want to be as wild as I feel
to be fearless in the face
of my own judgment.
But if I'm being truly honest,
what I want most is the promise of you.
You are deeply woven into the fabric
of everything I want my life to be.
It burns in me
this desire to love you
all the days of my life.

Quiet moments
with the ones we love.
That is our greatest anchor
in this life.
These are the moments
that hold us steady
keep us from completely
losing our minds.
These are the moments
that heal us
piece us back together
amidst the chaos.
Our whole lives revolve
around the stillness
and simplicity.
We linger in the silence
we find ourselves wrapped
in the comfort
that real love provides.
It is in this way
that we find the strength
to carry on.

Rights stripped away
in honor of life,
but whose?
Those who see in black and white
wield their power over us
ignoring the complexities of creation.
Deep in the heart
they argue over hearts
when they have none.
When women lose rights
to their own flesh and blood,
when healthcare is governed
by narrow-minded men
who only deal in political agendas,
humanity suffers.
Compassion is lost.
The ability to choose, demonized.
The pain, the chaos,
the uprising this will bring
makes me want to scream.

We were parked
atop the hill
in the black of night
watching the storm roll in.
Lightning dancing
across the sky
electricity surging
through our veins,
thunder growing louder
as our hearts beat faster.
Hand in hand
we felt the power
running through us
the wonder of
what was to come.

Children playing
running around the playground
faces covered as they go about
their usual activities.
I watch and wonder,
how will they remember
this version of the world?
How will this define
who they become?
Heartbreaking to see
a generation stalled
their childhood normalcy
taken away.
I watch and wonder.
What will they remember?
What meaning will they find?
How will they carry on?

It's a cycle we can't control
a natural rhythm
we can't escape.
It feels brutal
and yet beautiful
for there is unspeakable pain
mixed with a strange comfort.
Amidst the darkness
there is a silent understanding.
This is the way
it has always been.
Our lives are built upon
the ones we love and lose.

First comes the grief
the sadness
the tears fall on instinct.
Then comes the denial,
can this really be true?
Then slowly but surely
comes the inexplicable joy
the relief that the suffering
has come to an end.
Death is never easy
but learning how to release
with love and endure,
learning how to celebrate
the natural cycle of life
is one of the greatest
and bravest things we'll ever do.

It's that stormy time
of mystery and transformation
the bridge between
spring and summer.
The earth in constant
motion, so many elements
shifting around us.
The sky full of secrets
we look up and wonder.
The air thick
heavy with the intensity
of what's to come.
Most are longing for
the endless sun
but I cherish this time
intrigued by the turbulence
lured in by the darkness.

Shuffling through photographs
of days and memories past
the faces faded by the sun
the crinkled edges of what used to be.
When so much is lost along the way
it's hard to believe the things you had
were ever yours at all.
Perhaps time is what
leaves the biggest scar.
Time eventually takes
everything from us
and all we are left with
is what lives in our memory -
if we're lucky enough to have that.

We are endlessly drawn
to each other
this raw human connection.
So many forces of nature
can unite us
so many little moments
can piece us back together.
No matter how many times
we lose our way
we always find people
who bring us back
remind us how to heal.

Always looking back
because it's in our nature
to remember, to feel the
nostalgia, to cherish the memory.
The older we get
the richer our lives become
because we have so many
stories to tell, so many
pieces of ourselves to share
with the world.
There will always be
an inherent sadness
a subtle ache in us
where past times have lived.
But there is an even greater
exhilaration, a deeper gratitude
that we got to have
those experiences
and that we get to carry them
with us now.

A treacherous year
but it's already coming
to an end.
It still amazes me
how I ended up here.
Joy laced with grief
a fog that lingers
around every corner.
So much to celebrate
as my flames burn bright
but the scars I bear
will never fade.
Every step forward
I will remember
the losses
the sacrifices
the pain
that changed my life forever.
Life will go on
but we will always
carry it with us.

Finally at peace
eyes locked in a gaze
this is where I feel it.
This quiet knowing
this unwavering certainty
brings all the comfort I need.
Our eyes speak volumes
as we soak in this
fascinating silence.
Our souls drawn together
like magnets
no amount of pain
can keep us from this.
Here in the stillness
this is how we heal.

It's hidden in the
mundane moments
lingering in the little things.
The feeling I long for
the simplicity I desire.
It's what I've come to live for
in a world that has
re-charted my course
sent me running wildly
in a new direction.
Certainty may be fleeting
but it's not as hard to find
as you may think.
There's plenty of it.
Everywhere.
If you only know where to look.

I'll always remember this moment
wrapped in your embrace
looking up at the stars
the beginning of goodbye
without the promise of return.
I stand here loving you
as much as I always have
looking to the night sky
searching for a glimmer of hope
in the constellations.
Time has come to a halt
as we linger in the longing.
Here we surrender
sacrifice all we know
and let go of this love
to find out what it's made of.

Plagued by the demons
the monsters born
from the brokenness.
Pain popping up
little reminders on our phones
one after another.
Every day headlines
smeared with blood
read between the lines
and you'll find
that we are to blame.
The violence
the brutal crimes
the shameful enabling
of this scathing injustice
cannot continue.
The cycle has been endless.
Over and over we suffer.
So how do we find our way out?

Like a deep fog
it lingers.
Hanging in the air
thick and oppressive
clouding our vision.
It surrounds us
and no matter
which way we turn
there's no path in sight.
So we take off moving
hoping we'll eventually
see the other side.
But day after day
it lingers.

Where my feet meet the sea
and the waves come
rolling in endlessly
this is where I ask
my questions, and often
where I find my answers.
Looking into the vast beyond
I'm reminded how fragile life is,
but also how it carries on
despite the pain we feel from living.

Let go.

Accept.

There is peace here
if you're brave enough to feel it.

We are a collection of stories.
Words, imagery, sensations
shared around tables
repeated year after year
savored and remembered.
We are the people
we are surrounded by
the laughter we share
the tears that bond us
the conversations that unite us.
We may not realize it
but we are crafted in the telling,
and when we look back,
we see that our lives
have been built upon it.
We are a collection of stories.

We are so ashamed
of our humanity,
so sensitive about
the things that
make us fragile.
Vulnerability
seen as weakness.
Emotion
seen as embarrassing.
We hold it all in,
create an image that
is acceptable to the world.
But deep inside
we are all the same.
All struggling, all searching,
all wondering, all hurting.
All children of the same desires
but we are afraid to reveal.

The war rages on.
The war with government
the war with politics
the war with nature
the war with each other.
I am filled with fuel
I can feel my fire
raging within
ready to take on
whatever comes next.
But this is still
an exhausting path.
Brave as I may be,
my heart is still weary
grieving the losses
aching from this long
and painful journey.

Grateful for the darkness.
Grateful for the chaos.
Grateful for the layers
that were stripped away
so I could discover
what I'm truly made of.
I am a fire
in a world where people
are so easily extinguished.
I will carry on
knowing what matters most,
knowing that I carry within me
everything I need to survive.

My tears fall so easily
when you are in pain.
This life is hard
and there is no map.
Every person,
every journey
is unique.
Society will make you think
there are rules you should follow.
People will tell you
how they think you should live.
So much pain comes
from not knowing,
not being who you are.
We must each find
our own truth,
discover the wild within.
All I want is for
you to find your fire
and carry it like a torch.
Proud, confident, untamed.

Don't be afraid
to let it burn.
Don't be afraid
to watch the fire
and wait for it to burn out.
Have the courage
to sift through the ashes
because you never know
what you may find
hidden beneath the rubble.
Where there is destruction
there is always a new awakening.

Seems everywhere I turn
these days there is pain.
Pain in all shapes
and all sizes.
Everyone is walking
through their own
kind of fire,
yet we are all
one flame.
All burning with
the intensity of what
it means to be human.

You don't have to say it.
I can feel it.
I know.
Let it live in the
space between
let it grow stronger
let it become your
truth once again.
I will wait until you're ready.
Until you come back
into your own
until you understand
what we've always known.
I will be here
watching the fire
in your eyes
and waiting until
the time is right.

In a world of chaos
in a time of crumbling
and destruction
we must stand firm.
We must fight.
We must dissent.
We must speak up.
We must feel it all,
allow ourselves to
experience our full humanity.
We cannot be swayed
by the endless manipulations
and influences that surround us
and demand our compliance.
We must walk through the fire
and know that we are fireproof.

Why do we deny ourselves
the things we truly want?
Why do we repeatedly
extinguish the fire within us?
Every day we navigate
the world and are told
where to go, what to desire,
what to consume, who to follow,
who to be.
Whether we know it or not,
we are losing ourselves
slowly.
We are losing our humanity.
In a world that is unbalanced
in a system that is broken
we willingly play our part.
I refuse to play my part.
My discomfort, my anxiety,
my restlessness comes when I
deny my soul what it needs.
What I need does not come
from out there.
I exist only for the fire within.

Seems like my life
has become a roller coaster
of emotions, an experiment in
how to manage anxieties
that I've never had before.
Who I was before,
the life I had,
is gone forever.
Time to embrace
this change,
despite its chaotic origin
and the hardships
it will continue to bring.
Time to enter a new
phase and way of life.
Time to accept.
Time to heal.

It isn't us against them.
Human rights are human rights.
We should all want
the same thing.
When people with power
abuse it, hurt people with it,
they should be punished.
End of story.
No need for us to hate
an entire group
just because of
the sins of a few.
We should all be united
in the same fight for justice.
Only together
can we rise up.
Only together
can we find peace.

Words,
when crafted wisely,
can be wielded
like a sword.
Words hold such
great power to
change the world,
yet we are usually
so quick to take
hasty or violent action.
Perhaps the best
strategy is one that
requires skill and patience.
We take words for
granted, diminish their
significance, often because
we hear them from
careless mouths and
illegitimate sources.
But we must not forget,
when words are backed
by knowledge and truth,
when they come from a
place of wisdom and humility,
those are the words
that can save us.

I am continually amazed
by the ways that
human kindness
can save the world.
It's easy to get transfixed
by the bad news, get saddened
by corruption and greed.
But we cannot forget
that there are so many
others out there
serving humanity
what it truly needs.
Love.
Understanding.
Music.
Film.
Art.
Words.
Messages of hope.
We are not alone.
We are one human race.
Now is the time
to stand together.
To unite and win this fight.
Despite the pain
and chaos of this world,
human kindness
will always prevail.

For a woman
there exists
a silent scream
always buried
in her throat.
We women bear
the weight
the worry
the wonder
of the world.
A fire burns
within us,
for we are capable
of so much more
than the standards
that have been set.
We have dreams,
desires, passion.
All we want is a chance.
A chance to live.
A chance to choose.
A chance to be
who we really are.

Time is nothing.
Time is everything.
In a world that has
come to a standstill,
in a world where we
have lost control,
time takes on
new meaning.
It's ironic how fast
time is taking
things away,
and yet as a result,
we are actually
gaining time.
Time for simplicity.
Time for healing.
Time for change.
Time for renewal.
This change is painful
uncomfortable
unfathomable.
But we must be
brave enough
to forge a new path.
Be grateful for every
piece of our lives.
All the parts that
make us whole.
Time is nothing.
Time is everything.

No matter where you
are in the world,
I will always
carry you with me.
You are a part of
my soul, which is why
I will always hurt
when you hurt.
I feel your struggles
as if they were my own.
What a burden it is
to not be able to ease
your burdens,
how heavy I feel
knowing you are
being weighed down.

I have been deeply changed
by two unique souls.
I've had connections
most only dream of.
I've seen wonderful, sleepless nights,
long conversations, crazy rides,
and felt joy that has
brought me to tears.
I have found love
that has changed the
very fabric of my being
and allowed me to
realize my true nature.
How mysterious and beautiful
it is to be alive.

All the things
I took for granted
all the times
I could have loved you better,
oh how it haunts me now.
But the truth is
that I had to be
here in this place
standing still in the darkness
before I could finally see.
Some of life's greatest lessons
are learned
past the point of no return.

I stare into the fire
looking for answers
in the flames.
The soft glow,
the fiery movement,
here is where I find stillness.
I am still as I contemplate
the road behind
and the road ahead.
How do I carry on
while remaining most
true to myself?
I stare into the fire
as I wonder
what will keep mine alive.

I look across the
Scrabble board at you
and I take you in,
every inch of you.
You are deep in thought,
buried in your letters,
but I am in awe.
It doesn't matter
that we've been stumbling
just trying to survive
each day.
Here in this
beautiful calm
I remember
what we are
and I regret nothing.

I observe people
for a living.
I follow them around
capturing life's
important moments.
It never ceases to amaze me
just how profound
the little moments are.
The little moments
between
the big moments.
Perhaps the biggest moments
are the smallest ones.
Always occurring naturally
spontaneously
without any effort at all.
These are the moments
we live for
and yet we don't
even realize it.
It's these moments
that make us who we are

Your tears roll down
my cheeks
as you press your
face into mine
in the middle of the night.
Your words close the gap
fill the spaces
between our hearts.
It doesn't seem like much
but these are the moments
that mean everything.

When did our
basic human instinct
become judgment?
Criticism?
Hatred?
When did it
become so hard
to show compassion,
understanding,
love?
When children
have to fight
for their own safety,
we are failing.
We have failed.
Big changes
must happen,
but we must also
look within ourselves
to understand
how we let our freedoms
become this destructive.
There must be a way
to have the freedoms
we want without
letting them ruin us.
Can we ever truly be free?

There can be such a gap
between my inner
and outer life.
And it's when
they are disconnected
that the sadness sets in.
All of life
seems to be finding a balance
between who you are inside
and who you are to the world.

Becoming an adult.
It involves growing pains.
It forces you to reflect
on your past
so you can understand
how to better shape
your future.
You must realize
which parts of you
have carried over from
childhood, and which
parts have vanished
altogether.
To truly become
who you are,
you must accept
yourself for who
you once were.
You must face your
flaws, learn to love
all your imperfections.
You must embrace
uncertainty, for your
life is now completely
yours to live.
Allow yourself
to become.

Life is a funny thing.
Not knowing what to do.
Not understanding who we are.
Not always following the right path
or realizing our purpose.
And yet,
there's something unexplainable
that makes us want to
wake up every day
and just keep on living.
Even when we're a mess
and nothing makes any sense.
We keep going.
Somehow,
something makes us
keep on going.

It was her eyes
that drew him in.
It was the sweetness,
a radiance he'd never
seen before.
Deep wells full of love
and loyalty, a bravery
that inspired him.
He found home
in the way her gaze
lingered, in the way
it calmed his dark waters.

I've become keenly aware
of all the bluebonnets
growing everywhere.
I envy them.
They are allowed
to blossom and grow
and spread and be wild.
They are protected.
Everyone is supposed
to just leave them alone
and let them be
what they are.
They are completely free
to just be what they are.

To be
is to not be
anything at all.
To be
is to exist
because you are
who you are.

So full of life
just like the springtime
blossoming around me.
The air full of sweet,
delicious promises,
the flowers revealing
their forgotten beauty.
Looking forward to the sunlight
of the near and thrilling future,
my heart budding in ways
I never knew it could.
A sense of newness,
fresh starts, and easy beginnings,
there is simple joy
to be found in everything.

Our story is a complicated one,
but one thing has always been simple:
the way we care about each other.
We've been through everything.
Through the good and the bad,
for the worse or the better,
somehow we are able
to remain together.
Over the course of time,
you've had your way with me.
You wrecked me, you made me,
you healed me, you saved me.
From what, I don't know.
But you did.
You saved me.
Not the kind of saving
that we know as heroic,
but rather the kind of saving
that is long and gradual: a process.
A million little things
compiling over time,
slowly and subtly
changing my life.
My entire existence
has been altered because of you.
You seem to bleed
into everything I do.
Oozing, dripping, splattering,
across the canvas of my life.
No color can disguise you,
no tool can erase you.
Lingering with me,
like a beautiful, intriguing scar,

you will forever be
a permanent mark on my heart.

Moments come
and moments go,
what magic awaits,
you'll never know.
The universe is filled
with a million little wonders,
and the simplest moment
could change your life forever.
Big moments are special,
we plan them
and delight in them.
But the true beauty of life
is hidden in little moments
that occur in an instant,
and change us in ways
we never expected.

One of the most important
lessons in life
is to find the beauty in waiting.
So much of our lives
consist of waiting,
and too often
we waste this time
because we are too focused
on what lies ahead.
What a shame it is
to not take notice of the time we wait,
for you never know
what you could find
when you aren't even looking.
Waiting…
it doesn't have to be a burden.
Open your eyes
and choose to see
all of the possibilities
and take advantage of
every
single
moment.

To write
is to tap
into my soul
to pull water
from the deep, dark well
that resides inside me.
It can be
a difficult task
but without the water
I retrieve from the well
I could not survive at all.

We've laid down our weapons
ceased all our fire
and finally realized
what needs to transpire.
Simple words
are all it will take
because the lack of them
is what made us this way.

Affected so deeply,
I feel everything
with a painful intensity.
Just as the wind
can cool my skin,
so the sun can
burn it without warning;
and so I go through life
always wondering
but never knowing.

As my feet landed upon the warm, smooth sand,
I felt the ocean breeze tousle my long, brown curls.
I could see the deep blue waves rolling in with the tide.
The sky was fading from pink to yellow, yellow to orange;
the clouds were like wispy watercolor brush strokes.
The huge, glistening sun sank in the sky
and into the arms of the sea.
All was quiet, peaceful, and calm;
nothing could be heard but the symphony of the waves.
The cool water approached gracefully, caressing my bare
toes.
With every moist step, I watched my footprints
wash away with the waves.
I breathed in the fresh, salty air,
and breathed out all my troubles;
because here in the midst of indescribable beauty,
I had no reason to worry.
Every wave pulled me in
as though the ocean were calling my name.
The rest of the world ceased to exist
until there was nothing left
but the sand
the waves
and the setting of the shimmering sun.

Always judging
the path beneath my feet
as I look around and see
the journeys of others.
I love who I am
but am still guilty
of comparing my life
to those around me.
Should I have reached
this milestone
or that accomplishment?
My greatest joy can be
found when I sink into
the present moment
and release all thoughts
of what I'm supposed to be.

Some days I wish I could hide away
in the safety of an elevator
enclosed by four secure walls
where nothing can harm me.
I'll ride up and down
all day long
and the movement will be soothing.
But I know that the security
isn't going to last,
because sooner or later
the doors will slide open
and I'll have to face life again.

Laying down
on this merry-go-round
eyes to the sky
looking for the reasons why
I keep moving
but I'm going nowhere.
The answers so unclear
I'm paralyzed by fear
hoping for a sign
or the stars to align
so I can understand
where to go from here.
Sunrise, sunset,
but I can't forget;
it lives in my mind
I can't leave it behind.
I'm defined by the one thing
I don't know how to give up.

In this moment
it's not about getting back
what I've lost.
It's about being
where I am
remembering that the
greatest joy can
come from sorrow.
Perspective is everything
and sometimes the best views
come from the free fall.
You just have to be
brave enough
to let go.

It's part of my daily routine
putting on the armor
that no one can see.
The way I carry myself,
confident and sure
an eagerness for life.
Who would suspect
the weight that I carry?
I am split in two -
half joy and half sadness
every day walking the line
one step at at time
hoping against all odds
that the love within me
will survive.

Like ocean waves
it crashes over me
the saltwater burning
my open wounds.
What was once a
place of calm
is now a hurricane
that I can't escape.
Doomed to remain here
as the power of the storm
takes over me
I close my eyes
and hope to survive
as the darkest night of my life
closes in.

Pull me from the darkness,
you know where to find me.
Kiss me at the seams
let your breath linger
as you piece me
back together.
Without a word
you know who I am
you know where I wander
and how to bring me back.
Stitch me up
with your gentle hands
hold me firmly
in the broken places.
With your alluring eyes
guide me back to the light.

We have always been a storm
for we are both
children of the rain.
We've always been
slaves to the thunder
filled with lightning
just hoping not to
hit the ground when we strike.
But despite the intensity,
we are also the calm
after the worst has passed.
That is where we find our beauty.

I crawl into bed
and tuck myself in
with my sadness.
As I slip into the quiet darkness,
the silence reminds me.
I hear the echoes
and succumb to the void.
Nothing has ever
ached this deeply.
I lay here lifeless
waiting for sleep to
take me,
free me from this nightmare.

Soft and sensitive
vulnerable but alive
radiating with love
that burns so bright.
She feels everything
so much more
than is ever revealed.
She only wants to love
overflowing with words
that sometimes have
nowhere to go.
There is no greater pain
than her love denied
but she molds every hurt
into a torch that she
carries through the darkness.
She is resilient and brave
determined and focused
a champion of truth
a warrior for love.

Rage is splitting me open
as grief courses through my body
running all the way to the core.
Pain invading my body
until I don't know where
one feeling ends
and another begins.
It's all-consuming
and it's too late
to close the floodgates.
Nothing left to do but
surrender, let the adrenaline
protect me so I can't
feel the damage,
let my body do
what it needs to heal.

I am powerless,
a slave to the waiting.
Still I stand
as the world
swirls around me.
How I long to be
in motion, to have a
direction to run in.
Everything still dark
the weight still heavy
I close my eyes
and envision the light.
I anticipate my moment.
Please let it come.

She hides within the walls
of her own silence
and no one even suspects.
Everything appears fine
but it's all just
smoke and mirrors.
A sleight of hands
an innocent smile
and she's got you seeing
what she wants you to see.
How does she do it?
The magic lies
in the shadows
in the subtle movements
that no one can see.
She may have everyone fooled
but she cannot fool herself.

Some days I find myself
exhausted by culture,
the trends and rules we follow
mimicking and repeating like parrots
that which we see on social media.
Before we know it
we are stuck in cycles
unable to think for ourselves
unclear of why we do
the things we do.
We dissolve into our screens
and come out the other side
perfectly polished
begging for likes and follows
unaware of how we
lose ourselves in the process.
When was the last time
you asked yourself -
Who am I really?
What do I want the world to see?

I see her in photographs
I recognize her
and yet she is
a stranger
a memory almost forgotten.
I used to be her
before life took the reigns
and led me into
the great unknown.
Such an innocent smile
a look of pure happiness
she was free
so sure of who she
wanted to be.
She is gone now
but wisdom has taken her place
I look up to her
for she is a spirit that
time cannot erase.

We think we know
we think we are invincible
we think we understand
how our lives should unfold.
But then death shatters
what we think we've figured out,
what we think we know of life.
Whether it's sudden
or we know it's coming,
it breaks us just the same.
But maybe that's where
we find beauty.
Maybe what we must learn
what we must love
about life and death
lives in the dark corners
around the jagged edges.
Maybe the best of life
is how we mend.

I walk willingly
into the flames
knowing that I can
become part of the fire
rather than fighting it.
I can adapt,
take on the form
of whatever life brings
because it will not destroy me.
I have learned that
surrendering
is the ultimate strength.
Knowing when to surrender
is how we survive.

I do not wish to be numb.
I do not crave the ways
in which people
silence their demons.
I long to feel
no matter how deep
the ache
no matter how wide
the grief.
I do not wish for pain
but I will take it
as it comes,
sit with the sadness
as it shows me
who I am.
We hurt as deeply
as we love,
and triumph or not
the pain is a sign
that we are alive.

Haunted by time
always watching the
clock tick
planning every minute.
Always stuck waiting
for the fulfillment
of my desires
holding on for outcomes
that may never come.
I will the clock
to bend to my control
but oh how I bleed
in the process.
Chained at the wrists
by the idea
that there's never enough
while my wildest dreams
await me
if I can let go
and give it all up.

It's so hard
to admit you're suffering.
How do you show
the world
your broken places?
No amount of searching
will give you answers.
You must always find
the truth within
Even when it's the
hardest place to look.

Always drifting
just out of grasp
I ache for it
but can't attain it.
Just when I find
a place to land
the ground beneath me
shifts again.
Safety is not what
it used to be
not the home that
used to protect me.
Every day I wake
the storm rages on
and I march on
through the downpour
just hoping to find my way.

I've memorized your scars
traced the lines
between them
become an expert
on the things you carry.
I've learned how to hold you
in the deepest hours of the night
how to soothe your mind
back to sleep.
I value the map
of your soul
and see beauty
in the jagged paths
that you've traveled.
We always meet here
in the same hiding place
ready to challenge
each other's demons
and love each other
back into the light.

So much light ahead.

Finally.

I can feel the sun
on my face.
I will run toward it
with joy and relief,
but the ache in me
will linger.

I was not made
to let go
I will never be the one
to walk away.
I will hold on
knuckles tight
and fingers bleeding
until the rope
is cut from my hands.
It is in this way
that I love
in this way
that I live.
Loyal
no matter what
it costs me.

The embers remain
glowing for now
but waiting to see
what will become of them
is maddening.
Any moment
a spark could
set them ablaze
or they could
fade into ash.
Always on the edge
of life and death
but no one can
tell the difference.

Two little girls
bouncing up and down
eager to see you.
You turn on the stereo
and the excitement builds.
Your brilliant smile
our wide eyes
gazing at you in wonder.
I twirled around
feeling the music
through my whole body.
I locked eyes with you
matching your gestures
as you moved to the beat.
I am grateful for the
songs and memories
that will last a lifetime.
Grateful for a father
whose passion for living
still lives in me.

I need to rediscover
my body, remember
all the things
I love about her.
I need to appreciate
all the things
she can do
despite the things
she cannot.
Perfection is not meant
to be achieved.
We are meant to
bear scars, marks,
lines on our skin
of a life well-lived.
I need to be kind,
listen to what she needs,
for I must evolve with her.

So much of what people say
are things they've been
conditioned to believe.
Anger rises in me
responses sometimes slip
through my lips without warning
but then I remember
the role that culture plays.
I remember the things
I'm unlearning
while those around me
continue to play their parts.
I need not defend
the life I have chosen,
the rhythm that works for me.
I have stepped outside
the box and am self-aware
in a world that functions
in neat little boundaries.
I will not apologize
for living my truth.

Wandering.
Wondering.
Waiting.
Wishing for the past
and the future
at the same time.
Wanting to wake up
in the present
and find the restoration
I've needed for so long.
What will come
from this pain?
How will I rise?

Surrounded by support
I lean on those I love
but am still left lonely.
We may share
a collective pain,
but healing is
an individual experience.
No one can save me.
I get help along the way
but I must face
the journey alone.
From sun up
to sun down
is an achievement.
And for now, that's okay.

I'm okay.
I'm not okay.
Both are hard to admit.
I've never felt anxiety
that runs this deep.
It courses through me
and some days
I'm paralyzed.
A stranger in my own body.
So many have healed
so many have moved on.
But I remain here
sifting through the remains
picking up the pieces
searching for the life
that is to come.

Everything seems to make sense
from behind a camera
or with a pen in my hand.
When I am creating
I am certain of who I am,
grateful for how
I came to be here.
But it's when my hands
are empty that I feel it.
The loneliness.
The self-doubt.
The questions that are
never-ending.
Always walking the line
between passion and pain.

The things I hide
the things I suppress
are burning me
from the inside out,
but I let them.
I let it hurt
I suffer in silence
because I don't want
to create a conflict.
I don't want to fight.
I just want to survive.
So what do I do
with the burdens I carry?

We've always been
opposites that attract
pulled together
like magnets that
can't resist.
No matter the time
or distance
we have always felt it
even when we
can't say it.
Over and over
life breaks us
but even when we run
we always find our way back.

I long for the darkness
intrigued by its many dimensions.
The secrets, the sensations,
the sounds.
I love to feel everything
even when it hurts.
The mystery, the madness,
the majesty.
I will always be wandering
here, drawn to the danger,
called to the adventure.

Every day
is a struggle to breathe
when everywhere I turn
is something that could suffocate me.
Sometimes all I want
is to be able to take
just one step
without falling.
I want to stand
on solid ground
just for a moment.
Every day
I try to persist,
try to keep this sadness
from swallowing me whole.

I've always longed
to be good enough,
strived to fit into a mold
that wasn't meant for me.
I was taught how to succeed
how to work hard
how to find my place.
And yet,
I realize now that
I will never fit in.
I am good enough
just as I am.
I am meant to live
for more than
the things I'm told
I should be.
I have always been more.
I will always feel the urge
to run wildly
into the flames.
And I will.
Against all odds.
This is who I'm meant to be.

Everyone keeps moving forward
as I keep moving back
all my hopes and dreams
are under attack.
Spinning in circles
wondering where I went wrong
wishing I could've saved myself
if I hadn't been so young.
But maybe I was supposed to
end up here.
This is the lesson I have to learn.
Maybe it's beyond what I can see
the life that is meant for me.
Is it time for a new dream?

In the quiet
in the isolation
in the emptiness
I heard the sound.
Familiar, comforting.
But this time, I heard it clearly.
My voice.
The only one I've ever had,
the one that has always been there.
It is no longer muffled.
No longer drowned out
by useless noise.
I sink into it,
finding strength in the words
that define who I am.
In the darkness
in the pain
in the chaos
I have come alive.

As the cold night descends
I am wrapped in the warmth
of these nostalgic melodies
filled with mystery and wonder.
I am reminded of the power
of music, the way it can
save me from anything.
I remember all the seasons past,
the joy that always finds me
year after year.
I savor the traditions
the rituals that make me whole.
I am a child again,
longing for the excitement
eyes wide and filled with hope.
This is the time of year
when I truly come alive.

It was never about
accepting you.
The moment we first
connected, I was yours.
All these years,
all these struggles,
it has always been
about accepting myself.
Letting go
and letting myself be.
You always lived
so unapologetically
and I admired that.
You've made me realize
I don't need blueprints,
I don't need plans.
The present here with you
is what matters.
Now more than ever.
Accepting this moment,
this me.
This us.
That is all it has ever been about.
And now, I understand.
There is no destination
for me to reach.
I am already here.

I watch the last bit of light
fade away,
the soft colors of the sky
melt into black.
The darkness surrounds me
like a cloak, and strangely,
it's comforting.
There's something about
the night that draws me in.
The night understands.
This is the time to unwind,
let go.
The night brings a freedom
that daylight will never know.
Here in the shadows,
here in the quiet,
I am allowed to feel.

It's taken me so long
to grow up,
so long to recognize
the cages that have
held me back,
kept me tame.
So many of the things
I thought I wanted
were not even my ideas.
Who am I when I strip away
what the world expects of me?
What do I truly want
when I silence the voices around me
and listen to my own?
I am finally learning
that this life is mine
and explanations and apologies
are no longer needed.

On the page
I craft my words well,
but on my tongue
my words are poison.
They leave my mouth
often without thought
or reason.
I long for the patience and ability
to control my thoughts
before they are spoken aloud.
I am a lover of words
but I do not want to
be reduced to ashes by them.

There is darkness
coming from every
direction it seems.
Everywhere I turn,
pain and uncertainty.
The chaos of the world
is an interesting backdrop
as I grapple with
my own challenges
and continue to travel
deeper into myself.
So much to reckon with.
So much still to learn.
All these different forms
of darkness that surround me
push me forward,
although I can't see the path ahead.
I'm sure the map
will reveal itself in time,
but for now I'm just wandering.
Wandering alone in the darkness.

Something in me
feels structurally different.
Something in my core
has changed.
It's interesting how
the times have shaped me.
How my instincts have shifted.
What used to matter to me.
What I've realized matters most.
Something in me feels new.
These changes
though caused by chaos
are exciting in a way.
There's a new version
of me to explore.
I know very little
of what the future holds.
All I know is
I'll never be the same again.

I am stuck
on a carousel
that won't stop turning
and I can't get off.
Time keeps going.
The world moves on
around me,
but I am not part of it.
I watch. I observe.
But I cannot join.
I will not join.
Maybe I can't get off.
Maybe I won't get off.
Maybe both.
What am I waiting for?
I don't know.
But for now I keep turning.
Frozen in time.
Watching.
Waiting.
Wondering.

Sometimes the problem
with my anger
is that others
don't feel it with me.
When I become
consumed
I want everyone
to feel the way
I do.
I feel everything
in a way unfamiliar
to most.
I just want people
to understand.

I long for the night
especially now
for the daytime
brings the memory
the reminder
of what I should be doing.
In the daylight
all I see is the life
I should be living.
The night, the darkness
offers solace
a place to retreat
to think
to process
to contemplate
to accept
to rest.
The night is a perfect
backdrop for all
my deeper feelings.
The night brings
a perspective
a type of wisdom
and self-discovery
that I need to survive.

Lay me down
show me the way home
worship my body
the way it moves.
Let us meet in the sanctuary
we've long forgotten.
Devour me here
take all of me
leave nothing left
but the hymns of our love
echoing off the walls
and guiding us
through the darkness.

I am hopeful.
I remain hopeful.
And yet some days
this anger consumes me.
Sometimes I am paralyzed
by a type of pain
I can't even identify.
I'm a generally happy person.
People know me
for my positivity.
So how do I explain
what I'm feeling underneath?

Panic Switch takes me back
to backroads riding shotgun
windows rolled down
sun streaming in
my arm dancing out
the window to the
rhythm of the music.
I can still feel
the warmth on my skin
see the smile on your face
the joy of those simple days
that felt infinite.
Just two kids
falling in love
content to wander
taking in every moment together
nowhere else in the world
we'd rather be.

Someone please show me
how to relinquish control.
So often I find myself
trapped in a glass cage
I have created for myself.
I imprison myself
holding on so tightly
to unrealistic expectations.
What is the point
of living this way?
Why do I always
distance myself
from the true freedom and joy
I seek?

"I still love you."
Four words
echoing through the night
a flicker of hope
in the darkness.
A confirmation
of what I've always believed.
The path forward
remains unknown
but this little confession
holds the possibility
of a love that could
be re-ignited
a chance of a new life
that could be
born from the ashes
of the past.
The journey continues on
but your declaration
will linger.
I still love you,
too.

I sat there so still
my heart racing
as your pencil glided
across the page
bringing my features
to life.
I sat there gazing
admiring you as
you worked,
the shape of your hands
your eyes as they
examined me
taking in every detail.
I could feel myself falling
drawn in by your
passion and patience
mesmerized by the way
you made me into art.

In the quiet
with the ticking
of the clock
I feel the weight.
The weight of responsibility
the weight of time
the weight of uncertainty.
My burden is that
I always want to
do things right
have everything
in order.
But life usually
doesn't work that way.
I'm often left
waiting...
unsure what the
next step will be.
Every day
one day at a time
I am learning to trust.
Learning to be patient.
But some days
like today
the weight feels so heavy.

Sometimes I feel a
burning inside me,
words like flames
dying to get out,
yet I'm so judgmental
of my own voice.
Sometimes I keep them
inside me,
try to smother them,
but I can never gain control.
Words aren't always
perfect.
They don't always
craft the perfect phrase
or thought
or story.
Some days they
spew out of me,
messy in all their
imperfection.
And that's okay.
I have to learn
how to set myself free.

There is something within
every one of us
something we dare not
show the world.
We all have that
part of us, that mysterious
part that calls us
moves us
pulls us toward passion.
How it manifests
depends on me.
Depends on you.
This piece I love
to hide, but crave
to reveal.

Control.
I've always been
a control freak.
I am well aware
it is both a strength
and a weakness.
I've figured out how
to use it for
so much good,
crafting it like a skill.
And yet, sometimes
I lose control by
exerting too much.
Control.
I use it as a
sword and shield.
It's always a battle
trying to find
just the right balance
between good
and evil,
a fine line between
too much
and not enough.

If I am to be yours
I want you to feel it
in your bones.
I want that voice inside
to scream my name
so I can feel it
in the silence.
If I am to be chosen
please choose me freely
embrace me with
your wild knowing
and long for me
with certainty.
If you are to be mine
I will love you all my life.

In the soft glow
as my hand stroked you softly,
I could feel it
in my bones.
This is my purpose.
This is what I have to give.
Unconditional
unwavering
love.
Love that meets the darkness
and is not afraid.
When you cannot
carry your torch
I will carry it for you.
Although sometimes you must
venture off alone,
I will always be here
to light your way home.

We admire stained glass windows
all their brilliant shapes and colors
the stories they tell
the beauty of the whole
when the light shines through.
Works of art born
from the shattering of glass
broken pieces crafted
into something new.
A reminder that
beauty can come
from brokenness.

You really want
to know me?
To love me?
Then you must
read my words.
The words I pull
from deep within,
the words born
from the darkness
and the light
in my soul.
For me,
the truth comes out
in writing.
I feel
in letters
and ink.
I have a voice
that only exists
on the page.
Very few
have ever
experienced it.
But I love you.
I love you truly.
So I have given you
the key.
Read me.
Understand me.
This is who I am.

Love is both knowing
and not knowing.
Love is faith.
Equal parts choice and forgiveness.
It requires surrender,
patience, endurance.
Love holds us
and lets us go
for it is both freedom
and security.
Adventure and home.
Absence and presence.

I will say it in all the
ways I know how.
I will let it linger
until it takes root
and makes a home
in all the places
you've never felt it.
I will step back
let you find your way
and watch as you bloom
into what you were
always meant to be.

It's magnetic
the way your eyes light up
when you're immersed
in something you love.
You don't even know
how your passion radiates
drawing me in
over and over again.
For the rest of my days
I want a front row seat
I want to feel the joy
as you chase your dreams.

So many words
scattered across the years
hand-written and typed
etched into the fabric
of my being.
The telling of our story
is my greatest work of art
and no matter what happens
our love will live on forever.

Everything in me yearns for you
craves this shared life
longs for the roads
that we could travel.
It is part of my being
the way that I love you
effortlessly and certainly
a desire that will burn
for a lifetime.

What a great distance
we have traveled
running wild through the years
feeling every joy
conquering every storm.
It's a great honor
to experience a love like this.
A love that's raw and real,
imperfect but just what we need.
Some days we forget
where we came from
and lose sight of the road ahead,
but in these quiet moments
I close my eyes and remember.
I see you the way you always were
the way I've always loved you.
It all comes rushing through me
and I feel it in my soul.
We still carry this truth.

See it sprawled out
in front of you
all the words unsaid
promises unfulfilled
pieces scattered
yearning to be gathered.
You sit in the midst of it all
paralyzed by all that
you've lost in this life
all the love that
was stolen.
If you could only understand
that love is a choice
and it will always
live in you
then you could rise
and damn,
what a force you would be.

I'm tired of talking
of drowning in these
endless words
that pull us under
like quicksand.
Take my face in your hands
taste my aching lips
lean into the ancient language
of flesh and bone
body against body
and let yourself wander
where you dare not go.
Danger lies ahead
but so does truth.
Surrender to the rush
feel it all and feel it now
have the courage to become
all that you long for
all that you've lost.

Into the cold water we descend
and we can feel all our pieces
coming alive again.
Close your eyes
and turn back the clock;
see the nights we fell in love
in these very waters
remember the way the world
felt around us as we
surrendered to the joy
of those endless summer nights.
Let the water wash away
everything but the truth
and let us rise from it
ready to begin anew.

The world is so quick
to blow out your flame
but they will not win.
I have seen your light,
I have felt your warmth,
your flame has guided me
through many dark nights.
Don't worry, my dear.
I will forever keep re-igniting
your flame and holding
you high for all to see.
You were meant to be
a fire.
You lit mine,
and I will spend a lifetime
keeping yours alive.

It's the moments of joy
the tastes of pleasure
the aliveness permeating my skin,
these are the things
I long to share.
The light and the love
every bit of goodness
I can squeeze out of this life.
It all means nothing
without your hand in mine
and that lingering gaze
that feels like home.

We look in the mirror
and see the truth
of who we are
of who we've always been.
We see all that we long for
all that is already ours.
What if we are not lost
what if we were always
meant for this path?
All the winding roads
have led here
to the place where we
can surrender to the mystery
let go of what holds us back
and realize that all we
ever needed was
love.

The look in your eyes
the intimate words
the calming silence.
The mundane moments
the simple statements
that reveal the truth.
I collect them like snapshots
pin them on the walls of my mind
daily reminders of
a love worth fighting for.

I still remember
that first moment,
that first kiss,
an explosion of fire.
Our lips touched
and we could not
be separated.
In an instant
we become something
new and beautiful.
This love was
set in motion
and there was nothing
we could do
to stop it.
That night will
burn brightly in
my memory forever,
for it was the beginning
of everything.

A pipe full of dreams
fuels the flame
but what are we left with
when it bursts?
One explosion
scatters all our pieces
and we are left
surrounded by smoke
searching for embers
among the ash
hoping we can
keep them alive
just long enough
to find a way to survive.

You are the forbidden fruit
the apple on the tree
that I'm not supposed to pick.
But the more unattainable
you become
the more I long for you.
Oh how I crave the scent
the sweetness
the taste of you.
With resistance comes
intoxicating desire.
You are always there
just within my grasp.
I linger in the shadows
the temptation to sin
growing deeper.

At the core,
you and I
are the same.
I was drawn to you
because your fire
resembled mine.
The beginning was simple,
we ignited quickly
and our flames
could not be separated.
You and I have
always been
like a fire,
growing, burning,
spreading wildly,
refusing to be
extinguished.

I watch you remember
see it all come flooding back
the memory of who we were
the love we built
and the realization
that not much
has actually changed.
We grow up
we face life
we crawl our way
through the years
and get lost a little
along the way.
But all we have to do
is remember.
This love has
always been within us.
We are still those people
if only we choose to be.

I feel it in the
quiet moments,
unspoken truths
the ties that
bind us together.
Like a hurricane,
at the core of this chaos
there is a certain calm,
an unexplainable force
that holds us together.
Despite what surrounds us
I'll put my faith
in this calm
and the power it has
to save our lives.

Endless hours spent wandering
those small town streets
just two kids falling in love
imagining what our lives could be.
The magic of teenage romance
the highs and lows
the ecstasy rushing through our veins,
even then we knew
our lives would never be the same.
So young and naive
we dreamed of forever,
little did we know
we could never be together.
We couldn't have predicted
all that was to come;
we are still destined for each other
but were never meant for love.
I'll always cherish
that chapter in time
and be forever grateful for
the ways you changed my life.

I want to resurrect
the essence of our youth,
be re-invigorated by the
playful energy that
once sustained us.
It's been a rough couple years
and we've forgotten
the joy from which
we were born.
When you're young
you think the lust for life
will never end,
but as you grow older
you understand that desire
must be carefully cultivated.
Let's take off running
with reckless abandon,
take all that we've learned
and re-discover
all that we love.

It's an undeniable hunger
this craving I have for you.
The way you enter a room
the way your hair falls
around your face
the charming energy
you bring to any space.
It's no wonder
people are drawn to you.
They can feel it too.
The life force
the radiance you exude.
You are an enigma
I hope to spend
the rest of my life unraveling.

For me you'll always be
25 years old
in a white t-shirt
driving stick in that
Ford F-150
down back country roads
those brown eyes
full of adventure.
I'll always be
19 years old
riding shotgun
in your passenger seat
looking over at you
in admiration
willing to follow
wherever you lead.
It will always be us
running wild
untouched by time
two souls falling in love
and coming alive.

I love you with the kind of
anticipation that snowflakes have
as they fall toward a cold, wintery street,
hoping that it will be cold enough
for them to stick.
What sheer innocence
a snowflake has,
not knowing if it will survive
upon the ground,
and yet it falls anyway.

As day bleeds into
night, and night bleeds
into day,
time feels like
a straight line.
Where things used
to ebb and flow,
where there used to
be peaks and valleys,
now everything feels
the same.
This time, however,
is a gift.
Although the circumstances
are not ideal,
I am still grateful.
I can make this time my own.
I can feed my soul
in so many ways.
Time can sometimes feel
like a burden,
but it can also allow
for so much freedom.

If I could go back
to the beginning
I would do everything
just the same.
I'd fall in love
just as recklessly
and run toward you
with abandon.
I'd make all the
same mistakes
for every little choice
has taught me
how to love you
more truly.
We wouldn't have
a love this deep
if it had been easy.
Every scar holds
a beautiful truth
and nothing has ever
felt more real
than me and you.

I am impatient
and stubborn,
wildly frustrating
at times.
I know this.
But I will love you
with sincerity
you've never known,
share my passion
with you
like a story you'll
want to read over and over.
You can trust me
with your life
your shadows
the fragmented pieces
that make you
who you are.
Take my hand
and know that
you are home.

So many nights spent
falling in love
in the green light glow
discovering each other
piece by piece
fears falling away
beneath those sheets.
We were an unexpected match
and yet we connected so effortlessly.
The love story of our lives
flames erupting in the night
I found everything I'd ever wanted
lingering in those passionate eyes.

With winter on the horizon
I fall with the leaves
ready to let go
and surrender to the inevitable
changes of the season.
I anticipate the ritual
hibernation, the chance to
get back to my roots
and rest once more.
Weary from the heat
the endless sun
I welcome cooler days
and longer nights
filled with mystery
for the darkness has always
led me where I need to be.

Like a broken record
stuck spinning
singing your name
on repeat,
how I long for you
to lift this needle
and release me.
Dust me off
flip me over
and start my sweet melodies
once again.
Let me be the song
that soothes your broken soul;
close your eyes
and listen
as I call you home.

I close my eyes
and we're poolside
descending into the water
illuminated by moonlight.
Bodies light and magnetic
pulling each other in
without hesitation.
I can still feel
your soft lips
gliding across mine
so simple and effortless.
Wrapped around you
water trickling down my skin
I felt my world shift
as I let this love begin.

Sometimes just looking
at you sets my
skin on fire.
It takes very little
to ignite this passion
within me.
Just one look
and my mind starts
imagining all the
ways that I can
make love to you.
I have always
felt this way.
That is why I've
always known.
Deep down, in spite
of everything.
It's you.
It has always been you.

I feel it pulling
across the distance
intensifying the space
between us.
This desire steadfast
like the moon,
wherever we are,
it's there.

Like stained glass
you scatter your colors
across the surface of me
you cast your light
across the deep shadows.
I look up at you
and bask in the glow
letting your patterns
dance across my skin.
I am a reflection of all your pieces,
I hope you can see
how radiant you are.

Spin me round
let the music carry us
pull me into you
let me feel your heartbeat.
In this way it began,
so simple, yet so deep;
we fell into sync so quickly.
I look at you now
as we sway to the sound
and I'm so amazed
at the way I love you,
the elation I feel
after all this time.

So many stories
written upon my skin.
So many memories
living beneath the surface.
You have illustrated your love
everywhere you've touched.
I am your canvas
and you have made me into art.

Hold on.
Let go.
Close your eyes
and follow the
beating of your heart.
Dissolve.
Release.
Listen to your breath
as it guides you.
Surrender.
Discover.
Find me in
this exquisite stillness.

This vulnerability
this union in raw form
what a gift it is
to be what we really are.
We've never had guards
we've always shared
this sensitivity.
We co-exist in such
a natural state
unafraid to bare everything.
We can strip down
to the core
and know that this love
will carry us.

You are a fire,
which is what I've
always loved about you.
The way you light up
my life, set my soul ablaze.
The way we burn together,
beautiful and alive.
But with this intensity
there is always risk.
Always a chance
I'll burn out, be left
with the ashes.
And yet, I carry on.
Dancing in the flames.
Welcoming every sensation.
Finding peace in the space
between danger and delight.
I hope our flames are never separated.

We need the sensation
the chill that runs through us
igniting our cells
bringing us to life.
We long for the shiver
the rush from fingertips
traveling across
the landscape of our skin.
We crave the lips
that eliminate the space between,
the touch that elevates
takes us beyond ourselves.
This desire is endless
and so are the ways we find it.

To love is to learn how
to persist through the pain
to walk through the fire
to endure the longest nights
to do whatever it takes
to keep walking side by side.
Love can only be understood
when it is tested,
when you're willing to risk
everything you have for it.
To love is to move in
the same circle over and over
but to find you are stronger
every time you come back around.

The midnight hour
has become my favorite
when we curl up
our bodies resting
gently together.
No matter where the
days take us,
we always meet here.
The way we touch
the way we slip
into the darkness,
our hearts beating
softly in unison.
This feeling has become part of me,
and I don't ever want to live without it.

"We don't need to be
like we used to be,"
you said.
"We can be even better."
That is the beauty
of this love.
We are always moving
forward together.
Always finding new
ways to love each other.
I know you so well,
yet you still find ways
to surprise me.
We can look back at who
we were with fondness.
We can enjoy so many
sweet memories.
But nothing holds us back.
We live every day,
no regrets.
It doesn't matter
how much time has passed.
We are still so fascinated
with each other.
I still find ways
to fall in love with you
every single day.

Let me absorb your pain
let me feel it with you.
Let me in so we can
sit in the darkness
and feel the depth
of our humanity.
This is the place
where you find
who you are.
But you don't
have to do it alone.
Let me stay.
Let us share this darkness.
Let us come alive.

"Our love is strong,"
you whispered to me
as we were falling asleep,
"We can get through this."
Yes, my love.
We can.
When we lay in bed,
your arms wrapped
around me,
the world disappears
and I feel safe.
In this time of
chaos and pain,
in the face
of the unknown,
I am so grateful
to have you.

Something about you
makes me
surrender completely.
I look into your eyes
and I am willing to
give you everything.
I reveal all my pieces,
lead you into my darkness,
and you go willingly.
You welcome my
rough edges because
you have them too.
I love the way we can
hold each other,
creating a comfort
we both need.
We've figured out
how to mend each other
at the broken places.
That doesn't mean it's
always easy,
but we always show up
for each other.
That's the way it's
always been.
We love each other
in every moment
of joy, every moment
of pain, every moment
of destruction and discovery.
We love each other
and we surrender completely.

I just can't seem to
find words
to describe what
it is about you
that draws me in
so intensely.
Even when I find
myself questioning,
wondering,
pondering the nature
of our love,
something in me
still knows it's true.
Something in me
knows.
I search for words
to define it,
because that is how
I understand the world.
But perhaps real love
is indefinable.
Maybe all that matters
is that we feel it.
We feel it
and we know.

Let me touch you
let me penetrate
your soul.
Let me paint
a thousand colors
on your skin with
my warm, inviting fingers.
Let me take away
your burdens,
let me lighten your load.
Let me kiss you
until your pain
washes away.
I know how to love you.
All you have to do is
let me.

I wish I could save you
from yourself.
And yet, I understand
so clearly how you feel.
You want so much,
the fire in you burns
so passionately,
yet you find that you
are the only one
standing in your way.
I know ultimately
that there's nothing I can do,
but I try anyway.
Maybe I try to save you
because deep down
I'm still trying to save myself.

As the day fades
into darkness,
some nights
so do I.
My mind escapes me
and before I know it,
I've lost control.
Things look so different
in the darkness,
and it is easy
to get lost.
I don't mean to hurt you.
I wish I could keep you
from the crossfire.
But when my heart
is overflowing,
sometimes there is no
stopping my emotions.
All I want is for you to see me,
love me in the darkness.

I love the way we meet,
coming together
so effortlessly;
we know the road
and it knows us
as we travel toward
our favorite destination.
I love the way we meet
knowing every inch
every twist and turn
as we become one.
I love the way we meet
here.
Here in the darkness.

Change you?
I could never change you.
Why would I even want to?
Don't you see
that I love everything
about you?
I love every flaw
every inch of darkness and light
every single imperfection
that makes up your
fiercely wild soul.
Change you?
I could never.
I want to run wild with you forever.

Loving you means
I will gladly take your pain
and feel it as my own.
I will absorb your pain
endlessly
and spend my life
looking for new ways
to heal you.

If you think you're not
good enough for me,
then you clearly do not
understand the effect
you've had on my life.
I once wrote years ago
that maybe you'd be
the one to transform me
into the person
I'm meant to become.
That is exactly what you've done.
Don't you see
that you've set me free?
You are a mirror to my soul
and by looking into you
so much has been revealed.

I will never forget
the way I loved you,
the adventures we had
the lessons you taught me.
There was a time
when it was just you and me,
so young and free.
We were just kids,
nothing to worry about,
no idea who we were
going to be.
A decade has passed
since we met,
and what a decade
it has been.
We've loved each other,
hated each other,
and everything in between.
We've grown up
taken our own paths,
but never let each other go.
I am so grateful
to still have you in my life.

I love watching you
and all the things
you love to do.
You have so many
talents, so many skills.
You pour your heart
into the things you love.
Your passion radiates
from you and I love
being in its path.

You lay awake
staring into the darkness,
the day long gone.
Your mind wide awake
your ghosts circling
your thoughts, keeping
you from sleep.
I lay next to you
looking for ways
to soothe your soul,
quiet your restless mind.
You roll over and touch me
spilling all your deepest
thoughts about life,
all your inner demons,
and my love for you
grows deeper.
Deeper in the darkness.

We are so many layers
deep in this love,
and yet still
we go deeper.
There's always more
to discover,
more pieces of you
to admire.
You have really
mystified me
over the years.
This love has evolved
in ways I could have
never dreamed.
You broke all
my expectations
and it has been
the best thing for me.
Real love isn't about
finding the person that
meets your expectations.
It's about finding the person
who makes you realize
that you can have a life
far beyond any expectation.

I will always be here
to remind you endlessly
how wonderful you are.
How intelligent
how brave
how kind
how resilient
you are.
Don't you realize
there aren't many
people like you?
Like us?
It's no wonder
you struggle to fit in.
The world can be cruel
to people like you.
But please don't ever be
less than everything you are.
As I have always said,
you are a fire.
Be a fire.

Eucalyptus fills the air
a familiar and calming scent.
The rain trickles steadily
outside the window.
I see you in the low light
explore the shape
of your body
as you peel layers
off of mine.
We reach for each other
as we have a thousand times
eager for this sacred union.
I pull one last bobby pin
and my curls spill
around your face,
you pull me in
I close my eyes
and everything falls
right into place.

We escaped into the trees
descended into the creek,
with your hand in mine
we left the world behind.
We became part of the wild,
and I saw it in your smile,
there is so much to see
out here in the serenity.
It was so quiet
so peaceful,
no one in the world
but you and me.
Every cell in my body
felt magnificently alive
as I fell in love with you
and this magical place.

We cannot go back.
But we can retrace our steps.
Remember all the little
things along the journey
that made us into
who we are today.
Remember our scars,
our evolution, our healing.
We may be older,
we may be different
versions of ourselves,
but it's important to not forget
how we got here.
We must remember
why we fell in love.
Why we are in love.

The moon like a spotlight
on the dark shadowy fields
our cold hands
interlocked as one.
The stars so bright
as we wandered through the night
your eyes looking sweetly
into mine.
The world was quiet
no one but me and you,
you stood there silently -
and you were beautiful.

We do not get
infinite chances
we are not promised
any length of time
with the people we love
the things we hold
most dear.
We have no road map.
No destination to reach.
Take the leap.
Love harder.
Speak now.
Be brave.
Fight for what matters.
All we ever have
is this moment right now
to give our lives meaning.

Don't worry about me.
I am no victim.
I live with no regrets.
I have felt truly alive
in many brutal and beautiful ways.
No longer will my fear
of the unknown
dictate my happiness.
I have sat in the silence.
I have felt the knowing.
Cultivating my own strength
is my superpower
and I will trust in the truth
of what I know now -
I am enough.
So much more than enough.

About The Author

Taylor Juarez is a poet and filmmaker based in Austin, Texas. Inspired and encouraged by her mother and grandmother, Taylor discovered a love of writing at an early age. In high school and college, she began writing poetry and song lyrics. Taylor attended St. Edward's University in Austin, Texas, and graduated with a BFA in theatre.

Writing has helped Taylor metabolize her inner and outer experiences and find her truth. She explores what it means to be human through her raw, emotional poetry. When she's not writing, Taylor runs her own film company. In addition to writing and filmmaking, Taylor enjoys indulging in Grey's Anatomy, baking, and listening to her vinyl collection.

Facebook: www.facebook.com/blackinkmess
Instagram: @blackinkmess